Riley waved the girls behind a tree trunk. They watched as she pulled a pair of black sunglasses from her fanny pack.

"Sunglasses?" Nancy asked.

"Not just any sunglasses, Nancy," Riley said. "These sunglasses once belonged to . . . Eric Stanley!"

Nancy, Bess, and George stared at Riley. Then they began to shriek.

"Eric Stanley?" Nancy exclaimed. "Where did you get them? Where? Where?"

"Eric came to a mall in my old neighborhood a few months ago," Riley explained. "To sign his new CD."

"You *saw* him?" Bess gasped.

"Eric forgot his sunglasses on the table when he left," Riley went on. "So I took them. . . ."

The Nancy Drew Notebooks

Available from Simon & Schuster

THE
NANCY DREW
NOTEBOOKS®

#67

The Singing Suspects

CAROLYN KEENE
ILLUSTRATED BY JAN NAIMO JONES

Aladdin Paperbacks
New York   London   Toronto   Sydney

❧ ALADDIN PAPERBACKS
An imprint of Simon & Schuster Children's Publishing Division
1230 Avenue of the Americas, New York, NY 10020
Copyright © 2005 by Simon & Schuster, Inc
All rights reserved, including the right of reproduction in whole or in part in any form.
ALADDIN PAPERBACKS, NANCY DREW, THE NANCY DREW NOTEBOOKS, and colophon are registered trademarks of Simon & Schuster, Inc.
Designed by Lisa Vega
The text of this book was set in Excelsior.
Manufactured in the United States of America
First Aladdin Paperbacks edition August 2005
10 9 8 7 6 5 4 3 2 1
Library of Congress Control Number 2004109871
ISBN 1-4169-0087-X

The Singing Suspects

1
Rule of Cool!

We're on the case," eight-year-old Nancy Drew sang. She was holding the handle of a jump rope like a microphone. "So we're in your face!"

George Fayne and her cousin Bess Marvin stood on either side of Nancy. They held pinecones in front of their mouths and sang along: "We're the Spy Girlz!"

Nancy, Bess, and George were best friends. But this summer they were even more. They were a singing group. Today they were in the park, practicing for a big contest on Saturday!

The contest was part of the River Heights

Summer Celebration hosted by Mayor Stone. It was just for kids.

The name of Nancy's group was the Spy Girlz. That's because Nancy was the best kid detective in River Heights. She even had a blue detective notebook where she wrote down all her suspects and clues when she was working on a case.

"We're the Spy Girlz!" the friends sang again. They dropped down on their knees and shouted, "And we're watching *you*!"

Riley McArthur cheered as Nancy, George, and Bess bowed. Riley was in the girls' third-grade class at Carl Sandberg Elementary School.

"Can you take me with you to the Eric Stanley concert?" Riley asked. "Please?"

Nancy smiled. "Only the contest winners get tickets to Eric's concert," she said. "And we haven't won yet."

"Eric Stanley!" Bess swooned. She grabbed her heart and fell on the grass.

Eric was the girls' favorite teen singer. He had brown hair and brown eyes and a new song called "Rock My Socks!"

"What if we *don't* win?" Bess asked.

"Look at all the kids we're up against!"

She pointed to the others practicing in the park. Their friends Rebecca Ramirez, Molly Angelo, and Amara Shane had a group called the Girly Girls. Jason Hutchings, David Berger, and Mike Minelli called themselves Bad Newz.

"They're pretty good," Riley admitted. "But you guys are the *coolest*!"

George shook her head. "We may sound cool," she said. "But we don't look cool."

"What?" Nancy asked with surprise. "But I'm wearing my cool new jeans!"

"And I've got pink glitter on my sandals!" Bess said. "Isn't that cool?"

"If you're Tinkerbell," George said. She looked around the park. "Something is missing. We should look more like . . . them!"

George pointed at the stage. A group called Triple T was practicing. Triple T stood for the eight-year-old Tuttle triplets—Darly, Marly, and Carly. The triplets went to a special school for kid performers in the town next to River Heights.

3

"We're three times the groove," the triplets sang. "So let's busta move!"

"Wow!" Bess said. "They're singing and doing cartwheels at the same time!"

"Their gum didn't fall out of their mouths either!" George said. "How do they do that?"

Nancy and her friends watched the triplets sing and dance on stage. A whole crowd of people had stopped to watch too.

"They might as well be famous already," Nancy said.

"Thanks to their mom," George said. "She's here every day handing out Triple T pictures, pencils, and buttons."

Nancy looked over at Mrs. Tuttle. She wore a tank top, hot pink pants, and high heels. Today she was handing out Triple T balloons!

"The girls will be signing the balloons after practice," Mrs. Tuttle called out. "No pictures, please. Unless you're from a magazine or a newspaper."

Jason, David, and Mike walked past the girls. Mike dropped a Popsicle wrapper on the ground and kept on walking.

"Litterbugs!" Bess called after them. "No

wonder you're called Bad Newz!"

"Blah, blah, blah!" Jason sneered.

Nancy glanced down at the wrapper. There was a picture of the triplets on it. and the words KEEP COOL WITH TRIPLE T!

"Maybe George is right," Nancy sighed. "Maybe we're not as cool as they are."

"Maybe we're lukewarm," Bess said.

"What can we do to make ourselves cooler?" George asked. "Stick on tattoos? How about hot pink streaks in our hair?"

"Forget the tattoos and the pink streaks," Riley said. "I have something that will make you so cool, you'll turn hot chocolate into chocolate ice cream!"

Riley waved the girls behind a tree trunk. They watched as she pulled a pair of black sunglasses from her fanny pack.

"Sunglasses?" Nancy asked.

"Not just any sunglasses, Nancy," Riley said. "These sunglasses once belonged to . . . Eric Stanley!"

Nancy, Bess, and George stared at Riley. Then they began to shriek.

"Eric Stanley?" Nancy exclaimed. "Where did you get them? Where? Where?"

"Eric came to a mall in my old neighborhood a few months ago," Riley explained. "To sign his new CD."

"You *saw* him?" Bess gasped.

"Eric forgot his sunglasses on the table when he left," Riley went on. "So I took them. And the rest is rock history!"

Riley handed the sunglasses to Nancy. Nancy couldn't believe she was holding Eric Stanley's sunglasses. They had a silver *S* painted on the side, and a long scratch across the right lens.

"The *S* is for Stanley," Riley said. "The scratch was there when I found them."

"Are you going to send them back to Eric?" Nancy asked.

"Eric probably has a zillion sunglasses," Riley said. "Besides . . . finders keepers, losers weepers!"

George turned to Nancy and Bess. "Wait until we tell the world we have Eric's sunglasses!" she said excitedly.

"Don't tell anyone!" Riley pleaded. "Then everyone will want them. Especially that fourth grader, Mindy 'Nosy' Spinoza!"

Mindy was president of her own Eric

Stanley fan club. Nancy, Bess, and George wanted to join . . . until they found out they had to spit on their hands and high-five at every meeting!

"What fun is having Eric's sunglasses if we can't tell anyone?" Bess asked.

But Nancy didn't want to worry Riley. "We won't tell if you don't want us to, Riley," she said. "And we promise to take good care of the sunglasses too."

"Good!" Riley sighed with relief.

Nancy, Bess, and George left the park. Riley stayed behind to jump rope.

As the girls walked up Main Street they took turns wearing the sunglasses.

"They feel big on me," Nancy said.

"I can make them tighter," Bess said, her blue eyes shining. "I can fix anything!"

"Sure," George teased. "As long as you don't get your clothes dirty!"

Suddenly a voice called out, "Get your lemonade here! Ice-cold lemonade!"

Nancy saw Andrew Leoni. Their classmate was sitting behind a small table. On top were a lemonade pitcher and a stack of small blue cups.

"Hi, Andrew," Nancy said as they walked over. "How many cups have you sold?"

"Zero! Zip! Zilch!" Andrew said. He threw up his hands. "I'll never get to buy a new skateboard at this rate!"

Andrew leaned back and sighed. "Why doesn't anyone want to buy my lemonade?"

"Maybe because there's a dead bug floating in it?" George asked.

"Whoops!" Andrew said. He scooped it out and flicked it aside. Then he smiled and asked, "Would you guys like some?"

"Eww! I don't think so," Nancy said. As she shook her head, Eric's sunglasses fell off. They landed on Andrew's table.

Andrew picked them up and said, "Cool shades. What does the *S* stand for?"

"It stands for Stan—," Bess began.

George clapped her hand over Bess's mouth. "For Spy Girlz!" she blurted out.

Nancy put the sunglasses back on. Suddenly she heard voices. They were singing: "We love you, Eric! Oh, yes we do. We don't love anyone as much as yoooou!"

"Great," George groaned. "It's Mindy 'Nosy' Spinoza. And her whole fan club!"

Mindy and seven other girls walked over. They were all wearing Eric Stanley T-shirts and hats. The littlest girl was Mindy's five-year-old sister, Ella. She was wearing Eric Stanley socks!

"Lemonade!" one of the girls cried. "That's Eric's favorite drink. Let's get some!"

As they walked closer Mindy began staring at Nancy. She stopped walking and began shouting, "Ohmigosh! Ohmigosh! She's wearing Eric Stanley's sunglasses!"

Nancy stared at her friends.

Oh, no! she thought. *How does she know?*

2

Rock-'n'-Shock!

How do you know they're Eric's sunglasses, Mindy?" George asked.

Mindy rolled her dark eyes. "Do I not have Eric Stanley Fan Club meetings in my clubhouse every other day?" she asked. "Do I not have all of Eric's CDs, towels, and bed sheets too?"

"And those are the sunglasses that Eric wears in our favorite poster!" said one of the girls. She had on Eric Stanley earrings. "They have a silver *S* on them. And a big scratch. Just like those have."

Andrew leaned over and whispered, "I'd believe them if I were you."

Nancy was worried. They'd promised Riley they would keep the sunglasses a secret. But how could they keep it a secret from the Eric Stanley Fan Club?

"Okay, what do you want for them?" Mindy asked. "We'll give you a wad of gum that Eric chewed. And spit out."

"Eww!" Bess cried.

"That's totally gross!" George said.

"Thanks, Mindy," Nancy said with a smile. "We want to keep the sunglasses."

Mindy narrowed her eyes. But then she shrugged and said, "Who needs the sunglasses anyway? We have a real dollar bill that Eric signed just for us!"

"Here it is, here it is!" Ella said. She pulled a dollar bill from her pink plastic backpack and held it up.

"Wow!" Bess said as they looked at it. "Eric Stanley did sign it!"

"Give me a break!" Andrew said. "Do you want lemonade or not? I'll give you eight cups for just a dollar!"

"We'll take it," Mindy said. She didn't take her eyes off Nancy. "Give them a dollar, Ella."

"Okay, Mindy!" Ella said.

Mindy tilted her head as she looked at Nancy, Bess, and George. "Aren't you guys in the singing contest?" she asked.

"Yes," Nancy said. "We're called the Spy Girlz. We're practicing tomorrow."

Mindy and the fan club left with their cups of lemonade. Andrew stuffed the dollar bill into his shirt pocket.

"Thirty dollars to go for the skateboard." Andrew sighed. "If those sunglasses were mine, I'd take them straight to the Rock On Café!"

"How come?" Nancy asked.

"The Rock On Café has tons of rock-'n'-roll souvenirs!" Andrew said. "They'd pay money for Eric's sunglasses for sure!"

"That's nice," Nancy said. "But these sunglasses are not for sale!"

The girls left Andrew and began walking to their houses.

"I can't wait to practice in the park tomorrow," Bess said.

"We have the moves" — George did a little dance step — "and the grooves!"

"And Eric Stanley's sunglasses!" Nancy said happily. "Triple T, watch out!"

Nancy skipped all the way home. She went straight to the kitchen and saw Hannah Gruen placing a sandwich on the table. Hannah was the Drews' housekeeper. She had been helping take care of Nancy since Nancy was three years old.

"How do you like my new sunglasses, Hannah?" Nancy asked. "Aren't they neat?"

"They'll be neater once I clean those smudges on the lenses," Hannah said.

"You can't clean them, Hannah!" Nancy gasped. She took the sunglasses off and placed them carefully on the table. "Those smudges were made by Eric Stanley!"

Nancy's Labrador puppy, Chocolate Chip, padded into the kitchen. She nuzzled her nose against Nancy's knee.

"When I was your age my favorite singer was Elvis Presley," Hannah said. "He sang a great song called 'Hound Dog'!"

"'Hound Dog'?" Nancy said. She smiled down at her own dog. "I bet you'd like Elvis too, Chip!"

Chip barked just as the telephone rang. Nancy hurried to answer it.

"Hello?" Nancy asked.

"How are my sunglasses?" Riley's voice asked. "Your dog didn't lick them, did she? You didn't drop them, did you?"

"They're fine, Riley," Nancy said into the phone. "What's up?"

"I'm visiting my grandparents' farm for a few days," Riley said. "But I'll be back on Saturday for the contest."

"Cool!" Nancy said. "You'll get to see me sing with Eric's sunglasses on."

"Take good care of them, Nancy," Riley's voice pleaded. "Don't wear them if you chew bubble gum. The bubbles might burst and stick all over the lenses."

"I won't," Nancy promised.

"And don't wear them if you do cartwheels," Riley said. "Or hang upside down on the monkey bars!"

"Don't worry, Riley!" Nancy said. "I'll take *very* good care of them!"

Nancy hung up the phone. Then she turned around and saw Chip. Her puppy

had jumped onto a chair and was sniffing the sunglasses on the table!

"Don't even think of chewing those sunglasses, Chip!" Nancy warned. "Those sunglasses mean more to Riley than I ever thought."

"Did you wear the sunglasses to sleep last night, Nancy?" Bess asked the next day. "Did you dream about Eric?"

"I didn't wear them to sleep," Nancy said. "But Eric was in my dream anyway!"

It was Thursday. Nancy, Bess, and George were in the park getting ready to practice. They were about to walk toward the stage when suddenly a boy's voice shouted, "Out of my way! Out of my way!"

The girls turned. Their classmate, Orson Wong, was being pulled down the path by six big dogs on leashes!

"It's my summer job!" Orson shouted. "I'm walking dogs for fifty cents apiece!"

"You mean they're walking *you*!" Bess giggled.

Andrew was in the park too. He was

selling lemonade to a tall man with silver hair. Nancy recognized the man.

"It's Mayor Stone!" Nancy said.

"He better not find any bugs in *his* lemonade!" George snickered.

The girls walked over to the stage. Mrs. Tuttle was standing near it. She was talking loudly and shaking her finger at Jennifer Butcher. Miss Butcher was the dark-haired director of the singing contest.

"What do you mean Triple T can't practice first?" Mrs. Tuttle was demanding. "My girls are ready. See?"

She pointed to the triplets. They had formed a three-girl pyramid on the grass.

"We're not ready for them, Mrs. Tuttle," Miss Butcher said. "Spy Girlz is scheduled to practice first, at twelve noon."

"Spy Girlz are good," Mrs. Tuttle said. "But not as good as my superstars!"

Darly sneezed from the top of the pyramid. All three girls fell in a heap!

"That's got to hurt," Nancy whispered. "Let's go over and say hi."

As they walked over, Mrs. Tuttle handed

18

water bottles to the triplets. The bottles had Triple T labels on them!

"Wow!" Carly said. She pointed to Nancy. "Those are the coolest sunglasses!"

"Where'd you get them?" Marly asked.

Nancy gulped. "Um—"

"They're our lucky sunglasses," George blurted out. "We can't sing unless one of us wears them."

"Really?" Mrs. Tuttle asked slowly. Then she smiled at the triplets and said, "Darly, Carly, Marly, mother has a plan!"

What plan? Nancy wondered as Mrs. Tuttle whisked her daughters away.

Miss Butcher's voice interrupted Nancy's thoughts. "Time to rock, Spy Girlz!" she called.

The three friends hurried onto the stage. George handed Miss Butcher the CD of their song. She popped it into a CD player and the music began to play.

"We're the Spy Girlz!" Nancy sang out. But each time she did a dance step, the sunglasses slipped down her nose!

I'd better take them off, Nancy thought. *Before they fall off and break!*

Nancy finished singing the song, keeping one hand on the glasses so they would not slip. Then she walked to the side of the stage. First she made sure the surface was clean. Then she carefully placed the sunglasses down on the stage.

"Let's run through the song one more time, girls," Miss Butcher called.

The music played. This time George did a cartwheel in the middle of the song.

"Best practice yet, girls," Miss Butcher said when they were done performing. "Good job!"

"Maybe Eric's sunglasses *are* good luck!" Bess whispered.

"The sunglasses!" Nancy remembered. She ran to the side of the stage. But when she looked down, she froze.

"Bess, George!" Nancy cried. "Eric Stanley's sunglasses . . . are *gone!*"

3

Sunglass Case

"Gone?" Bess gasped.

"Are you sure?" George asked.

Nancy brushed aside her reddish blond bangs to get a closer look. All she saw was a wet, ringlike stain.

"Maybe they fell off the stage," George said. "Let's check it out."

The girls jumped off the stage and looked around. There were no sunglasses!

"Maybe they fell *under* the stage," Bess said. She turned to her cousin. "Go ahead, George. Crawl underneath and look."

"Why me?" George asked.

"Because you're wearing jeans and a T-shirt," Bess said. "And I'm wearing a new ruffled miniskirt with white trim!"

George shook her head and her dark curls bounced. She got down on her knees and scurried under the stage. After a few seconds she crawled out empty-handed.

"No sunglasses," George said, standing up. "Just a lot of dirt!"

Nancy leaned against the stage and shook her head. "I promised Riley I'd take care of Eric's sunglasses," she said. "What could have happened to them?"

"You guys," Bess said, "maybe somebody stole them while we were singing!"

"We were too busy singing to see anyone," George said. "But maybe Miss Butcher did."

The girls raced over to Miss Butcher. When they asked her about the missing sunglasses, she shook her head.

"I was too busy watching you perform to see anything fishy," Miss Butcher said.

Nancy, Bess, and George walked back to the stage.

"Somebody must have stolen them,"

Nancy said. "They couldn't disappear!"

"If you ask me," George said, "this smells like a mystery."

"A mystery!" Bess said. Her blond ponytail swung back and forth as she jumped up and down. "Are you going to solve it, Nancy?"

"I have to solve it!" Nancy said. "If I don't find those sunglasses by Saturday, Riley will never speak to me again."

The girls went back to the stage to look for clues. Nancy pointed to the ringlike stain on the wood.

"The ring looks like it could have been left by the bottom of a wet bottle or glass," Nancy said. "But it wasn't there when I put the sunglasses down."

"Whoever took the sunglasses could have been drinking water," George said.

Nancy nodded. "He or she might have put the bottle on the stage before taking the sunglasses," she said.

"Then it's a good clue!" Bess said, pointing to the stain. "Even if it is an icky one!"

Nancy grabbed her backpack and pulled out her detective notebook. But when she

looked for a pen she couldn't find one.

"Use this!" Bess said. She handed Nancy a bright pink pen. "Mrs. Tuttle was giving out Triple T pens, too."

"First water bottles and now pens!" George groaned. "What next?"

Nancy stared at George.

"The triplets were drinking from water bottles before we practiced," she said. "Maybe they took the sunglasses!"

"Why would they?" Bess asked. "We never told them they belonged to Eric."

Nancy tapped her chin with the pen as she thought. Then her eyes lit up.

"We told Mrs. Tuttle that the sunglasses were good luck!" Nancy said. "Maybe she didn't want Spy Girlz to have any luck and win the contest!"

"So she took the sunglasses," George said. "Or made one of the triplets do it!"

"And that could be the plan Mrs. Tuttle was talking about!" Nancy said.

"That's mean," Bess said with a scowl. "Especially for a mom!"

Nancy didn't like that their suspect was a mom either. But Mrs. Tuttle had a motive.

And Nancy knew that a motive meant a reason for doing something.

Nancy opened her notebook. On the top of the page she wrote WHO STOLE ERIC'S SUNGLASSES? On the next line she wrote MRS. TUTTLE. Underneath that Nancy wrote all the reasons she was a suspect: THE PLAN. THE WATER BOTTLES. SHE WANTS TRIPLE T TO WIN MORE THAN ANYTHING!

"Who else would want the sunglasses?" Bess wondered out loud. "No one knows they belong to Eric Stanley."

"Except Mindy Spinoza and her whole fan club!" George scoffed.

"Mindy!" Nancy exclaimed. "She wouldn't stop looking at the sunglasses!"

"And you told Mindy we'd be practicing in the park today!" Bess said.

"Me and my big mouth!" Nancy said.

"Write it down, Nancy!" George said, pointing to the notebook.

Nancy added Mindy's name to her notebook. Then she wrote SHE WANTS ERIC'S SUNGLASSES MORE THAN ANYTHING!

"Don't forget to write Jason, David, and Mike too," Bess told Nancy.

"Why would they steal a pair of sunglasses?" Nancy asked.

"Because they're Bad Newz!" Bess said with a nod.

Nancy didn't think the boys had done it. But she wrote down their names anyway.

"Now let's find the thief," Nancy said, shutting her notebook. "And the missing sunglasses!"

The girls looked for Mrs. Tuttle and the triplets. But their search turned up empty, so they decided to question Mindy Spinoza instead.

"Mindy lives on Byrd Street," Bess said. "I once sold Pixie Scout cookies to her mom."

The girls walked a few blocks to Mindy's house. There was no car in the driveway. No one in the front yard, either.

"Are you sure Mindy lives here, Bess?" Nancy asked.

"Does that answer your question?" Bess asked. She pointed to a tree in the yard. Carved into the trunk were three big hearts and the words "Mindy Loves Eric!"

"The tree house up there must be Mindy's clubhouse," George said.

The clubhouse was only six feet off the ground. It had a ladder leading up to a wide door.

"Maybe the sunglasses are up there," Nancy said. "Let's sneak a peek!"

Bess climbed up the ladder first. George followed her. Nancy was about to climb up when—

"Cheese and crackers!" Bess cried. She stood at the top of the ladder, staring into the clubhouse. "Omigosh!"

Bess backed away from the tree house.

"Climb back down!" she cried. "Go! Go!"

The girls scrambled back down the ladder.

"Give me a break, Bess!" George said. "What did you see in there? A ghost?"

"A snake?" Nancy asked.

Bess shook her head. Then she smiled a big smile and said, "I just saw Eric Stanley!"

4

Cyber Clue!

Eric Stanley?" George cried. "Now I know you're losing it, Bess!"

"It is Eric!" Bess hissed. "Go up there and see for yourselves. Go ahead!"

"I'll do it," Nancy said.

I know Mindy has Eric Stanley souvenirs, Nancy thought as she climbed the ladder. *But I didn't know she has Eric Stanley himself!*

Nancy reached the top of the ladder. She looked inside and gasped. Eric Stanley *was* standing inside. But when Nancy looked more closely, she began to laugh.

"It's a cardboard cutout of Eric," Nancy called back. "Not the *real* Eric!"

Bess and George joined Nancy in the tree house. They tapped the cardboard cutout.

"I think I saw this in the music store," Nancy said. "That's probably where Mindy and her fan club got it."

"Phooey!" Bess said. "I was hoping it was the real Eric Stanley!"

"Is that why you almost flew down the ladder?" George teased.

Nancy, Bess, and George got to work looking for Eric's sunglasses. They found some fun things—like Eric's guitar pick. They also saw a few gross things—like a clear box with a tissue Eric had blown his nose in! But they did not uncover Eric Stanley's black sunglasses.

"They still could have stolen them," George said. "Mindy's sister could be stashing them in her pink backpack."

"Just like that dollar bill Eric signed," Bess said.

"Maybe," Nancy said. "But we'd better go now, before Mindy catches us snooping around in her tree house!"

Nancy, Bess, and George headed for the open door. They looked down and Nancy gulped.

A big golden retriever was standing at the bottom of the ladder barking up at them!

"Woof! Woof Woof!"

"N-n-nice doggie!" Nancy called. "I have a doggie too. A much *smaller* doggie."

Bess started to shake. "What do we do?" she whispered.

"Are there any Eric Stanley dog biscuits up here?" George whispered back.

Nancy heard a car motor as a silver minivan pulled into the driveway.

"Busted!" George said.

Mrs. Spinoza stepped out of the minivan first. She pulled open the side door and Mindy jumped out. So did Ella and the rest of the fan club.

"Here, Erica!" Ella called to the dog. "Here, girl. Here, girl!"

The big dog ran toward Ella. And Mindy ran toward the tree house!

"Hey, hey!" Mindy shouted. "That clubhouse is for members only!"

"We don't want to join the club, Mindy," Nancy called down. "We just want to find Eric's missing sunglasses."

Nancy, Bess, and George scurried down the ladder.

"I didn't know they were missing!" Mindy said. "You don't think we took them, do you?"

"I don't know," Nancy said. "Where were you all at twelve o'clock today?"

"We just came back from Cedarville," a girl with an Eric Stanley stick-on tattoo said. "Eric was signing autographs at the mall there."

"The line was so long!" Mindy said. "He left before we saw him."

"But you already have Eric's autograph," Bess said. "On that dollar bill he signed."

All eyes turned to Ella. The little girl's face turned red.

"We *did* have the dollar bill," Mindy said. "Before Ella spent it somewhere."

"I can't remember where!" Ella said. "It could have been the pizza parlor, the toy store, the ice-cream—"

"Whatever!" Mindy said. She turned to

Nancy, Bess, and George. "You'd better leave now. We have a club meeting."

The club members spit on their hands. Then they high-fived.

"Gross," George murmured.

Nancy, Bess, and George left the Spinoza yard and went to Nancy's house. Nancy's dad was home early from work so he gave them milk and cookies.

"I'm not sure Mindy and her friends were telling the truth," Nancy said as she dunked a cookie in her milk.

"Yeah," Bess said, licking off a milk mustache. "How do we know they were in Cedarville? Or if Eric was signing autographs at some mall?"

"Need any help?" Mr. Drew asked. "I'm pretty good when it comes to mysteries."

Nancy smiled at her dad. He was a lawyer and often helped Nancy with her cases.

"I know how you can help, Mr. Drew!" George piped up. "You can give us permission to use the computer."

"Why the computer?" Nancy asked.

George swallowed a chunk of cookie. Then she smiled and said, "You'll see!"

Mr. Drew led the girls to the computer in the den. Nancy and Bess watched the screen as George went online.

"Just what I'm looking for," George declared. "Eric Stanley's official blog."

George clicked on the Web site. Soon a picture of Eric filled the screen.

"Cute!" Bess exclaimed. "Can I kiss the screen?"

"Don't make me gag, Bess," George said. "I want to find Eric's schedule."

After a few more clicks the girls were staring at Eric's summer schedule.

"Look. He did go to a mall in Cedarville today," George said. "He signed autographs from twelve noon until one o'clock."

Nancy remembered going to Cedarville with Hannah once.

"Cedarville is about a half hour away," Nancy said. "Mrs. Spinoza probably left River Heights at around eleven thirty this morning."

"And the sunglasses were stolen from the park at noon," George added.

"Which means Mindy was probably telling the truth," Nancy admitted.

The phone in the den rang. Nancy picked up the receiver and said, "Hello?"

"Nancy!" Riley's voice said. "Are Eric's sunglasses okay?"

Nancy gulped. She turned to her friends and mouthed Riley's name. George slapped her forehead. Bess bit her nails.

"Your dog didn't bury them in the yard somewhere?" Riley asked. "Did she?"

"No!" Nancy said. "Er-I've got to go, Riley. We have to work on our song!"

"But—," Riley started to say.

Nancy hung up. Then she turned to Bess and George and said, "We'd better find those sunglasses. And fast!"

That night Nancy could hardly sleep. She couldn't stop thinking about Eric's sunglasses. When Nancy finally did drift off, she dreamed about the missing sunglasses!

"Time is running out, you guys," Nancy told her friends the next morning. "We have to question Mrs. Tuttle today!"

The girls were in the park again to practice for the contest. But Nancy had only one thing on her mind—to crack the case before Riley returned.

"What about the boys?" Bess asked. "Aren't they suspects too?"

"I still don't think the boys did it, Bess," Nancy said.

"Yeah," George agreed. "We can't blame them just because they're pests."

Bess twirled her ponytail between her fingers. "Even if one of them happens to be wearing black sunglasses?" she asked.

"What?" Nancy and George asked at the same time.

Bess pointed to the stage. Jason, David, and Mike were strutting back and forth and singing.

"We've got gum on our shoes!" the boys rapped. "That's why we're Bad Newz!"

They wore baggy pants, loose shirts, and backward caps. But Jason was wearing something else that made Nancy gasp.

"Jason *is* wearing black sunglasses!" Nancy said. "And they look just like Eric's!"

5

Sour Power!

ancy!" George said. "I think I see something silver on the side!"

"I told you the boys took the sunglasses!" Bess said. "I told you so!"

Bad Newz slid across the stage on their knees as they finished their song.

"Way to go, guys!" Miss Butcher said. "You're done practicing for the day."

"Yo, dudes!" Jason declared. "To the monkey bars!"

The boys pounded knuckles. Then they raced toward the playground.

"Follow them!" Nancy said, breaking into

a run. But then Miss Butcher called, "Spy Girlz! You're up next!"

Nancy skidded to a stop.

"We can't—I mean—not now!" Nancy said. "We have to go to the playground!"

Miss Butcher put her hands on her hips. "The playground?" she asked. "How can you play when you have to practice?"

"It's not play," Nancy said. "It's work."

Miss Butcher looked confused. But then she said, "Okay. But don't be long."

In a flash the girls were at the playground. Jason, David, and Mike were heading toward the monkey bars.

"Jason Hutchings!" Nancy shouted. "You give me those sunglasses right now!"

Nancy expected Jason to keep on running. But he stopped, took off the sunglasses, and tossed them to Nancy.

"Knock yourself out," Jason said. "There are tons of these around!"

Nancy caught the sunglasses. "What do you mean?" she asked.

"Nancy!" Bess cried. "Look at the playground!"

Nancy's mouth dropped open. All of the kids on the swings were wearing black sunglasses! The kids on the seesaws were also wearing black sunglasses! So were the kids on the monkey bars!

"*Everybody* in the park is wearing black sunglasses!" Nancy cried.

"They can't *all* be Eric's!" George said.

Nancy stared at the sunglasses in her hands. They were black just like the missing pair. But instead of a silver *S*, they had a silver *T*!

"T . . . for Triple T," Nancy said slowly. "Now I get it!"

"Get what?" George asked.

"Mrs. Tuttle's plan!" Nancy said. "When she saw me wearing sunglasses, she wanted to make another Triple T souvenir!"

"So she made Triple T sunglasses," Bess said. "And gave them to everyone!"

"That explains her plan," George said. "But what about that ring-shaped stain we found on the stage yesterday?"

"The triplets were drinking from their own water bottles," Bess reminded her friends.

A pink Frisbee glided over Nancy's head. She whirled around. Mrs. Tuttle was pulling Frisbees out of a box and flinging them in the air.

"Get your Triple T Frisbees here!" Mrs. Tuttle shouted. "They're all signed by Darly, Marly, and Carly!"

"Not again!" George groaned.

"This is our chance to question the Tuttles," Nancy whispered. "Come on."

Darly, Carly, and Marly were signing each Frisbee before their mom tossed it.

"My hand hurts!" Darly said.

"And we want to go on the swings!" Carly complained.

"Faster, girls," Mrs. Tuttle said with a smile. "It's good practice for when you're big stars!"

"Mrs. Tuttle?" Nancy asked as they walked over. "May we ask you something?"

"Of course you can have a Triple T Frisbee!" Mrs. Tuttle said, smiling. "And I'll be handing out Triple T yo-yos later. Would you like some of those, too?"

"No, thank you," Nancy said. "We just want to know where you were yesterday—"

"Spy Girlz!" Miss Butcher's voice cut in. "Time to practice. Right now, please."

Phooey! Nancy thought. *I'll never get to question the Tuttles!*

The girls passed on the Frisbees. But George took a Triple T water bottle from Mrs. Tuttle.

"George!" Bess complained as they ran to the stage. "Whose side are you on?"

"I'm thirsty!" George said.

The girls filed onstage. They practiced their song and dance. When Nancy, George, and Bess were finished Miss Butcher clapped her hands.

"Good job, Spy Girlz," Miss Butcher said. "I'll see you tomorrow for the big contest!"

Tomorrow? Nancy thought with a gulp. *That's when Riley will be back!*

The girls climbed down from the stage. Nancy noticed that the ring-shaped stain was still there!

"That's weird," Nancy said. "Water wouldn't leave a stain like that. It would have disappeared when it dried."

"Unless the stain didn't come from a water bottle," Bess said.

George took a sip from her Triple T water bottle. Then she placed it on the stage, next to the stain. She lifted the water bottle and compared the mark it left with the other ring. "The stain isn't from a Triple T bottle," she said. "This bottle's way bigger!"

"Which means"—Nancy sighed—"Mrs. Tuttle and the triplets are innocent."

Nancy took her notebook out of her pocket. Then she crossed out Mrs. Tuttle.

"No more suspects," Nancy said. "What do we do next?"

"How about ice cream?" Bess asked.

Nancy listened. She could hear the bells on the ice-cream truck jingling as it rolled into the park.

The girls raced to the truck. Nancy and George bought Fudgsicles. Bess bought a box of Bon Bons. They were about to toss their wrappers in the trashcan when George pointed inside the barrel.

"It looks like Andrew was selling lemonade in the park today," George said. "There's one of his cups."

Nancy stared at the small blue cup.

"Lemonade!" she said. "Maybe the stain was made by a lemonade cup!"

"There's only one way to find out," George said, reaching into the trash can.

"Eww!" Bess said, wrinkling her nose. "How can you touch garbage?"

George picked up the cup and smiled. "Like this!" she said.

The girls ran back to the stage. George placed the cup on top of the stain.

"A perfect match!" Nancy declared.

"What if Andrew Leoni is the thief?" Bess gasped. "He was selling lemonade in the park the day the sunglasses vanished!"

"Why would Andrew take them?" George asked. "All he wants is a new skateboard."

"That's it!" Nancy cried. "Andrew wanted to sell Eric's sunglasses to the Rock On Café. So he could get money for a new skateboard—"

"Woo-hoooo!" a voice shouted.

The girls spun around. A boy on a skateboard was charging down the path. As he got closer, Nancy gasped.

"It's Andrew Leoni!" Nancy said. "And he's riding a skateboard!"

6

Flips and Tips!

Maybe he sold enough lemonade to buy a new skateboard!" George said.

Nancy narrowed her eyes and said, "Or maybe he sold Eric Stanley's sunglasses!"

Andrew waved as he whizzed by.

"Andrew, stop!" Nancy called. "We want to ask you something!"

"No way, Nancy," Andrew called over his shoulder. "I'm on a roll. Woo-hoooo!"

Just then Nancy saw Orson. He was walking his dogs across the same path!

"Andrew!" Nancy cried. "Look out!"

Nancy and George dropped their Fudgsicles and covered their eyes. Bess clutched her box of Bon Bons.

"Whooooa!" Andrew yelled. As he swerved his skateboard flipped out from beneath his feet—and Andrew flipped onto the grass!

The dogs barked as they pulled Orson over to Andrew. They surrounded him and began licking his face.

"Cut it out, you guys!" Andrew cried.

"Why don't you look where you're going?" Orson said, pulling back his dogs.

Nancy, Bess, and George ran over to Andrew. He was wiping dog slobber off his face with his sleeve.

"Yuck!" Andrew said. "Dog spit!"

"Andrew," Nancy said. "How did you get that skateboard?"

"The Rock On Café gave it to me," Andrew said, standing up.

"Because you sold them something that belonged to Eric Stanley?" Nancy asked.

"Sort of," Andrew said.

"Aha!" George cried. "You did steal Eric Stanley's sunglasses!"

"What are you talking about?" Andrew asked. "I gave them the dollar bill that Eric signed. The one the fan club had."

Nancy stared at Andrew. "How did you get that?" she asked.

"Mindy's sister used it to buy lemonade the other day," Andrew said. "I found it while I was counting my cash this morning."

George whistled between her teeth. "So that's what happened to that dollar!"

"It was mine fair and square," Andrew said. "So I gave it to the Rock On Café. And they gave me this cool skateboard."

"Instead of money?" Nancy asked.

Andrew nodded as he picked up his skateboard. "It once belonged to some other rock star," he said. "I think his name was Elvis something-or-other."

Andrew hopped on his skateboard. He adjusted his helmet, then zoomed away.

"Let's get permission to go to the Rock On Café," Nancy told her friends. "I want to see this dollar bill with my own eyes."

As they turned to go, Orson hurried over with his dogs.

"Wait up!" Orson said. He held all six

leashes tightly. "I heard every word you said!"

Bess popped a Bon Bons into her mouth. "It's not polite to listen to other people's conversations," she said.

"Neither is talking with your mouth full," Orson said. "Look . . . I have top secret information about the sunglasses!"

"The missing sunglasses?" Nancy asked. "What do you know?"

"Not so fast," Orson said. He looked at Bess and held out his hand. "Valuable information always comes with a price."

"You mean Bon Bons?" Bess cried.

"Give him one," George commanded.

Bess frowned as she handed Orson a Bon Bons. The dogs panted as Orson popped it into his mouth.

"Yesterday when I was walking my dogs," Orson said as he chewed, "the beagle sniffed out some black sunglasses. They were under a bush near the stage."

"Maybe they were Eric's!" Nancy said excitedly. "What did you do with them?"

Orson held out his hand and said, "That will cost you too."

"Give me a break!" George cried.

"Okay, okay," Bess said as she tossed Orson another Bon Bons.

"Now what did you do with the sunglasses?" Nancy asked. "Tell us!"

"I did what any honest kid would do," Orson said. "I brought them over to the lost and found."

"Did the glasses have a silver *S* on them?" Nancy asked excitedly. "Did they?"

Orson held out his hand again.

"You want it?" George asked. She grabbed a couple Bon Bons from the box and threw them over Orson's head. "Then go get it!"

The dogs barked and dragged Orson across the grass to fetch!

"Stay! Heel!" Orson shouted.

"Come on," Nancy said. "Let's go to the lost and found and see for ourselves."

The girls raced to the lost-and-found hut. Mr. Kelly stood at the window. He had snowy white hair and a bright smile.

"Hi there, girls!" Mr. Kelly said. "What did you lose today? A jump rope? Roller skate? A tooth?"

"A pair of sunglasses!" Nancy said.

"Sunglasses, huh?" Mr. Kelly said. "A pair was turned in just this week."

The girls jumped up and down while Mr. Kelly ducked beneath the window.

"I hope they're Eric's!" Nancy said.

Mr. Kelly stood up wearing goofy sunglasses decorated with green plastic palm trees. "Are these the ones?" he asked.

"No," Nancy sighed.

"How about these?" Mr. Kelly asked. He held up a tiny pair of baby sunglasses.

Nancy shook her head. "Don't you have a pair of black sunglasses?" she asked.

"Let's see," Mr. Kelly said. He ducked beneath the window again.

"I think Orson was teasing us," Bess said. "Just so he could have my Bon Bons!"

But then—

"Well, what do you know?" Mr. Kelly's voice said. "Look what I happen to have here. Black sunglasses!"

Nancy stared at Bess and George. Could they be Eric Stanley's sunglasses?

7

Clues-Paper!

"Here they are!" Mr. Kelly said. He smiled as he held up the black sunglasses.

Nancy gasped. Not only were they black, the glasses had a silver *S* on the side!

Mr. Kelly handed them to Nancy.

"They've got to be Eric's!" Nancy said. But when she slipped the glasses on, she frowned. "Everything looks so . . . fuzzy."

"There's no scratch on the lens, either," Bess said. "They can't be Eric's."

"They look exactly like the missing pair!" George said. "I don't get it!"

"Me neither," Nancy said. "But they could be a good clue."

Mr. Kelly gave the girls permission to borrow the sunglasses.

"As long as you bring them back tomorrow. I don't think anyone will claim them before then," Mr. Kelly said.

The girls found a bench to sit on. Nancy opened her notebook and wrote her new clues: 1) THE LOST-AND-FOUND SUNGLASSES LOOK JUST LIKE ERIC'S. 2) ORSON FOUND THEM BY THE STAGE.

"By the stage," Nancy said. She stared down at her page. "Maybe the person who lost these sunglasses thought Eric's were his."

"You mean the thief took Eric's sunglasses by mistake?" Bess asked.

"They look so much alike," Nancy said. "And whoever did it, must have a name that starts with an *S*."

"Susie . . . Sam . . . Stanley?" Bess said.

"Samantha . . . Sydney?" George said.

The girls thought of names as they walked through the park.

"I give up!" George said. "And the singing contest is tomorrow. I'm going home to practice our song."

"Me too. I want to pick out my coolest clothes for the contest," Bess said. "If we don't have Eric Stanley's sunglasses, we'll have to look as cool as we can."

Nancy stared at Bess and George. Were her friends giving up on the case?

"Who says we won't have Eric's sunglasses by tomorrow?" Nancy said. "This case isn't over yet!"

But as Nancy walked home she wasn't sure. *What will I tell Riley if I don't find the sunglasses?* she wondered.

Nancy spent the rest of the afternoon studying her detective notebook. She had no more suspects. Just a pair of strange sunglasses that looked just like Eric's!

"Time to ask Daddy," Nancy told herself. She carried her notebook and the sunglasses to the backyard. Mr. Drew was busy barbecuing burgers. He was wearing an apron, but still had stains on his sleeves!

Nancy giggled. Her dad was always getting spots on his clothes.

"What's up, Pudding Pie?" Mr. Drew asked as he flipped a burger in the air.

Nancy showed her dad the sunglasses

they'd gotten from Mr. Kelly. Then she told him about the lemonade cup stain.

"It sounds like you're on the right track, Nancy," Mr. Drew said.

"It's too late, Daddy," Nancy said. "Riley will be back tomorrow. She'll see what a big mistake I made and never talk to me again."

"Everyone makes mistakes, Nancy" Mr. Drew said. He nodded down at the grill. "Look how I just burned this burger!"

Mr. Drew used a spatula to lift the burger off the grill. "Hand me a piece of newspaper, please," he told Nancy. "So I can drop this crispy critter on it."

"Sure, Daddy," Nancy said. She found a newspaper on top of a chair. She was about to lift it up when she saw a picture on the front page. It showed Mayor Stone handing a trophy to the River Heights swim champ. He was wearing black sunglasses that looked just like Eric's!

"Daddy, look!" Nancy said. She ran to her father and showed him the newspaper.

"When was the last time you saw the mayor?" Mr. Drew asked.

"At the park!" Nancy said. "He was buying a cup of lemonade from Andrew."

"Lemonade?" Mr. Drew asked.

Nancy stared at her dad. Then she stared at the lost-and-found sunglasses.

"*S* for Stone!" Nancy exclaimed. "Daddy, I think I know who took Eric Stanley's sunglasses!"

"Where do you think Mayor Stone is?" George asked the next day.

It was Saturday. But the girls weren't getting ready for the singing contest. They were riding their bikes down Main Street and looking for Mayor Stone.

"My mom said he's cutting a ribbon for a new supermarket," Bess said as they pedaled. "But I forget which one."

"I bet that's it!" Nancy said. She pointed to a crowd of people standing in front of the Green Onion Supermarket.

The girls parked their bikes. Still wearing their helmets, they squeezed their way through the crowd.

Nancy saw a red ribbon stretched across the supermarket door. A man holding giant scissors stood in front of the ribbon. And next to him stood Mayor Stone—wearing black sunglasses!

"Mayor Stone!" Nancy shouted.

A woman dressed in a blue suit hurried over. Her pin read BELINDA JACKS, ASSISTANT TO THE MAYOR.

"Mayor Stone is busy right now," Ms. Jacks said. "If this is about the roller coaster you kids want in your schoolyard—"

"It's not about a roller coaster!" George said. "It's about—"

"It'll have to wait until the mayor finishes his speech," Ms. Jacks cut in.

"Speech?" Nancy gasped.

The mayor cleared his throat and began to speak: "When I was a boy, I loved going to the supermarket. I would gaze upon the shelves filled with cookies . . . bread . . . ketchup . . ."

"This is going to be the longest speech ever!" George groaned.

The mayor took off his sunglasses and rubbed his eyes. "That's funny," he said. "These are supposed to be special reading sunglasses. But I'm straining my eyes!"

Nancy pulled the lost-and-found sunglasses from her pocket. She began waving them in the air. "Try these, Mayor Stone!" she shouted out. "Try these!"

8

Spy Girlz Surprise!

Nancy ran forward with the sunglasses. Bess and George followed.

"I tried to stop them, Mr. Mayor," Ms. Jacks said. "But they were too fast!"

"It's okay, Belinda," Mayor Stone said. He took the sunglasses from Nancy. "Why, these look just like mine!"

Nancy held her breath as the mayor tried on the sunglasses.

"That's better!" Mayor Stone said. "I must have had the wrong pair!"

Nancy, Bess, and George cheered.

"What's going on?" Mayor Stone asked.

"We'll explain later, Mayor Stone," Nancy

61

said. "But for now, may we have those other sunglasses, please?"

"I don't see why not," Mayor Stone said, handing over the sunglasses.

Nancy, Bess, and George checked them out carefully. There was the silver *S*! And the long scratch!

"It's the *real deal*!" Nancy declared.

"I have to cut the ribbon now, girls," Mayor Stone said. "Can I help you with anything else?"

"Sure," George said. "About that roller coaster we want in the schoolyard—"

"Thanks, Mayor Stone!" Nancy said, pulling George's arm. The three friends squeezed their way back through the crowd.

"I can't believe it," Bess squealed. "We found Eric Stanley's sunglasses in the nick of time!"

"Speaking of time"—George glanced at her watch—"the singing contest is in one hour. We'd better get ready!"

Nancy slipped on Eric Stanley's sunglasses. She smiled and said, "I am so ready for this contest now!"

Nancy, Bess, and George rode their bikes to their houses. Nancy pulled on her cargo pants, black T-shirt, and orange sneakers. Then she put on the coolest thing of all— Eric Stanley's sunglasses!

Mrs. Marvin drove the girls to the park in her red minivan. They sang their song in the backseat. Then Bess gave Nancy a pink string with clips on both ends.

"I made it to hold Eric's sunglasses," Bess said with a big smile. "I told you I can fix anything!"

"Thanks, Bess!" Nancy said. "Now I'll never lose them!"

At the park the girls hopped out of the minivan. They raced to the stage. A crowd of people stood under a colorful balloon arch and a banner that read STARS OF TOMORROW SINGING CONTEST.

Nancy saw Mrs. Tuttle. She was handing out Triple T caps to everyone!

"There's Riley!" Bess said.

Riley ran over to the girls. She pointed to the sunglasses around Nancy's neck and said, "You took great care of Eric Stanley's sunglasses!"

"Well . . . ," Nancy started to say.

Suddenly Bess let out a shriek. She jumped up and down. "Omigosh!" she screamed. "Look who's a judge in the contest. Look!"

Nancy glanced at the judges' table. She saw Mrs. Oshida, the principal of Carl Sandburg Elementary School. Sitting next to her was Mister Lizard, the star of Nancy's favorite kids' TV show. At the end of the table Nancy saw a teenage boy with dark hair and eyes.

"It's Eric Stanley!" Nancy squealed.

All four girls shrieked at the tops of their lungs. They were still screaming when Miss Butcher walked onto the stage.

"Hey, River Heights!" she said. "It's time for the Stars of Tomorrow contest. So let's rock on!"

The Girly Girls were up first. They wore pink and performed a song called "Sweet as Candy." The next group to sing was Bad Newz. Their bubblegum rap got big laughs until Mike squirted a can of sticky string into the audience. Triple T performed next. They sang and did perfect cartwheels. Even after Carly's headband slipped over her eyes!

Finally it was time for the Spy Girlz! Nancy tried not to look in Eric's direction while they performed. But when they took their bows she sneaked a peek.

"Did you see that?" Nancy whispered. "Eric smiled at us!"

"I wonder if he recognized his sunglasses," George whispered back.

Four more groups did their routines. When the contest was over, the judges took some time to decide the best group. They wrote their choices on blue cards and handed them to Miss Butcher.

"And the winner for best singing group is . . . ," Miss Butcher began to say.

Nancy, Bess, and George grabbed hands and squeezed. Nancy could see Mrs. Tuttle whisking the triplets over to the stage.

"The Girly Girls!" Miss Butcher shouted.

Nancy was disappointed. But not as disappointed as Mrs. Tuttle.

"I demand a recount!" Mrs. Tuttle said. She yanked the Triple T hats off the judges' heads. Everyone gasped when she pulled off Mister Lizard's wig by mistake!

Nancy watched Molly, Amara, and Rebecca

run onstage. The Girly Girls were all smiles!

"Lucky ducks," George said. "They won front-row seats to Eric's concert."

"At least they're our friends," Nancy said as she saw another friend approach her.

"You guys rocked!" Riley declared. "But now that the contest is over, can I have Eric's sunglasses back?"

Nancy looked at Eric. He was busy listening to Mindy and her fan club.

"It would be nice if you gave them back to Eric, Riley," Nancy said softly.

"What for?" Riley asked. "As I said—finders keepers, losers weepers."

"There they are!" Mindy's voice shouted. "There are your sunglasses!"

Nancy and her friends spun around. Mindy was pushing Eric Stanley over to them. The rest of the fan club followed.

"You see, Eric?" Mindy said. She pointed to the sunglasses around Nancy's neck. "They were keeping them from you!"

"And we were just about to give them back," Nancy said quickly. "Right, Riley?"

"Um—right!" Riley blurted out.

Nancy took the cord off the sunglasses. Then she handed them to Eric.

"Thanks!" Eric said. "These sunglasses were a present from my dad."

Eric pointed to the lens. "And this scratch here," he said. "It was made by my favorite cat, Bonkers."

Wow, Nancy thought. *Eric missed those sunglasses more than we thought!*

"Do you all have tickets to my River Heights concert next week?" Eric asked.

"Like—duh!" Mindy said, smiling. "Everyone in the fan club has tickets!"

"We don't," Bess said. "We wanted to win tickets. But we lost the contest."

Eric grinned as he reached into his pocket. Then he pulled out four tickets!

"How about first-row seats?" Eric asked. "Right next to the Girly Girls!"

"No fair!" Mindy cried. "They're not even in the fan club!"

"But we're big fans," Nancy said.

Mindy turned away. "Guess we'll see you at the concert, then. Come on, Ella," Mindy snapped.

"Okay," Ella said with a smile. "Let's go talk to Mister Lizard!"

Nancy, Bess, George, and Riley couldn't stop smiling. As they walked to the ice-cream truck with their tickets, the triplets skulked by.

"We didn't win either," Darcy said. "I guess your sunglasses weren't so lucky after all."

Nancy looked at the ticket. She smiled and said, "Oh, yes they *were*!"

That night Nancy carefully placed her Eric Stanley concert ticket inside her desk drawer. She sat down at her desk, opened her notebook, and began to write . . .

Like Daddy said, everyone makes mistakes—even important people like Mayor Stone. I figured out something else. You don't need clothes or sunglasses to be cool. Take Riley, for instance. She said she'd never say "finders keepers, losers weepers" again. Now that is *way* cool!

Case closed!

COMING SOON:

Nancy Drew
and the ? Clue Crew

Nancy and her friends are
forming a detective club!

Join the Clue Crew on
their first case in
Summer 2006

COBBLE · STREET

has never been this much fun!

Join Lily, Tess, and Rosie on their adventures
from Newbery Medalist Cynthia Rylant:

The Cobble Street Cousins:
 In Aunt Lucy's Kitchen
 0-689-81708-8

The Cobble Street Cousins:
 Special Gifts
 0-689-81715-0

The Cobble Street Cousins:
 Summer Party
 0-689-83417-9

The Cobble Street Cousins:
 A Little Shopping
 0-689-81709-6

The Cobble Street Cousins:
 Some Good News
 0-689-81712-6

The Cobble Street Cousins:
 Wedding Flowers
 0-689-83418-7

Aladdin Paperbacks • Simon & Schuster Children's Publishing
www.SimonSaysKids.com

THIRD-GRADE DETECTIVES

Everyone in the third grade loves the new teacher, Mr. Merlin.
Mr. Merlin used to be a spy, and he knows all about secret codes and the strange and gross ways the police solve mysteries.

You can help decode the clues and solve the mystery in these other stories about the Third-Grade Detectives:

ALADDIN PAPERBACKS • Simon & Schuster Children's Publishing • www.SimonSaysKids.com

Ready-for-Chapters

She's sharp.

She's smart.

She's confident.

She's unstoppable.

And she's on your trail.

Still sleuthing,

still solving crimes,

but she's got some new tricks up her sleeve!

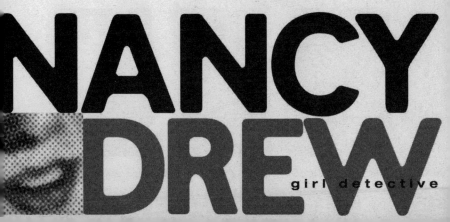

NANCY DREW

girl detective